CUMBRIA LIBRARIES

3 8003 04796 7823

D0794962

This Walker book
belongs to

〰〰〰〰〰〰〰〰〰〰〰〰

〰〰〰〰〰〰〰〰〰〰〰〰

*For Stephen – can't think of my childhood
without thinking of you*

A.

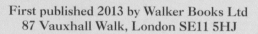

To Hannah and Max McFeely

L. T.

First published 2013 by Walker Books Ltd
87 Vauxhall Walk, London SE11 5HJ

This edition published 2014

4 6 8 10 9 7 5 3

Text © 2013 Atinuke
Illustrations © 2013 Lauren Tobia

The right of Atinuke and Lauren Tobia
to be identified as author and illustrator
respectively of this work has been asserted
by them in accordance with the
Copyright, Designs and Patents Act 1988

This book has been typeset in Caslon 3

Printed in Guangdong, China

All rights reserved.
No part of this book may be reproduced,
transmitted or stored in an information
retrieval system in any form or by any means,
graphic, electronic or mechanical,
including photocopying, taping and recording,
without prior written permission from the publisher.

British Library Cataloguing in Publication Data:
a catalogue record for this book is available
from the British Library

ISBN 978-1-4063-5468-3

www.walker.co.uk

SPLASH,
ANNA HiBiSCUS!

ATINUKE LAUREN TOBIA

WALKER BOOKS
AND SUBSIDIARIES
LONDON · BOSTON · SYDNEY · AUCKLAND

Anna Hibiscus lives in Africa.
Amazing Africa.

Anna Hibiscus is at the beach
with her whole family.
The sun is hot. The sand is hot.
The laughing waves are splashing.

Anna Hibiscus looks at the splashing waves.

Grandmother and Grandfather
are reading their newspapers.

Papa and Uncle Tunde
are talking to the fishermen.

Mama and the aunties
are plaiting their hair.

The cousins are busy too.

Joy, Clarity and Common Sense
are on their phones.

Benz and Wonderful
are playing football
with the beach boys.

Chocolate is burying
Angel in the sand.

"Angel!" shouts Anna Hibiscus.
"Come and splash with me!"
"I can't," says Angel. "I'm almost buried."

"Chocolate!" shouts Anna Hibiscus.
"Come and splash!"
"No," says Chocolate.
"You come and help me dig!"

But Anna Hibiscus does not
want to dig in the hot sand.
She wants to splash
in the laughing waves.
And she wants to splash
with somebody!

"Benz! Wonderful!"
shouts Anna Hibiscus.
"Come and splash with me!"

Benz and Wonderful are running
too fast to hear Anna Hibiscus.

"Kick the ball!" shouts Benz.
"Wondaful girl, kick'am!"
shouts Wonderful.

But Anna Hibiscus does not want
to kick balls on the hot sand.
She wants to splash
in the laughing waves.
And she wants to splash
with somebody!

"Joy! Clarity! Common Sense!
Will you come and play in the waves with me?"
asks Anna Hibiscus.

"No, no!" laughs Joy.
"We are too big now for playing," says Clarity.
"And we are too busy," says Common Sense.

Anna Hibiscus stamps away.
She wants to splash in the laughing waves.
And she wants to splash with somebody!

"Mama?" Anna Hibiscus asks her mother.

"First I need to finish plaiting,"
  says Anna's mother.
"And after that it will be time to eat."

  Anna Hibiscus kicks the sand.

"Go away to kick your sand,"
  says Auntie Joli.

"You will spoil the corn,"
  says Auntie Grace.

"Papa?" asks Anna Hibiscus.

"Don't interrupt," says Anna's father.
"Wait until I have finished talking."

Anna Hibiscus waits a long time.
But the men don't ever stop talking.

Anna Hibiscus looks at Grandmother
and Grandfather.
From underneath the newspapers
she can hear snoring.
Anna Hibiscus whispers,
"Grandmother? Grandfather?"
But there is no answer.

Anna Hibiscus looks around.
There is nobody left to ask.

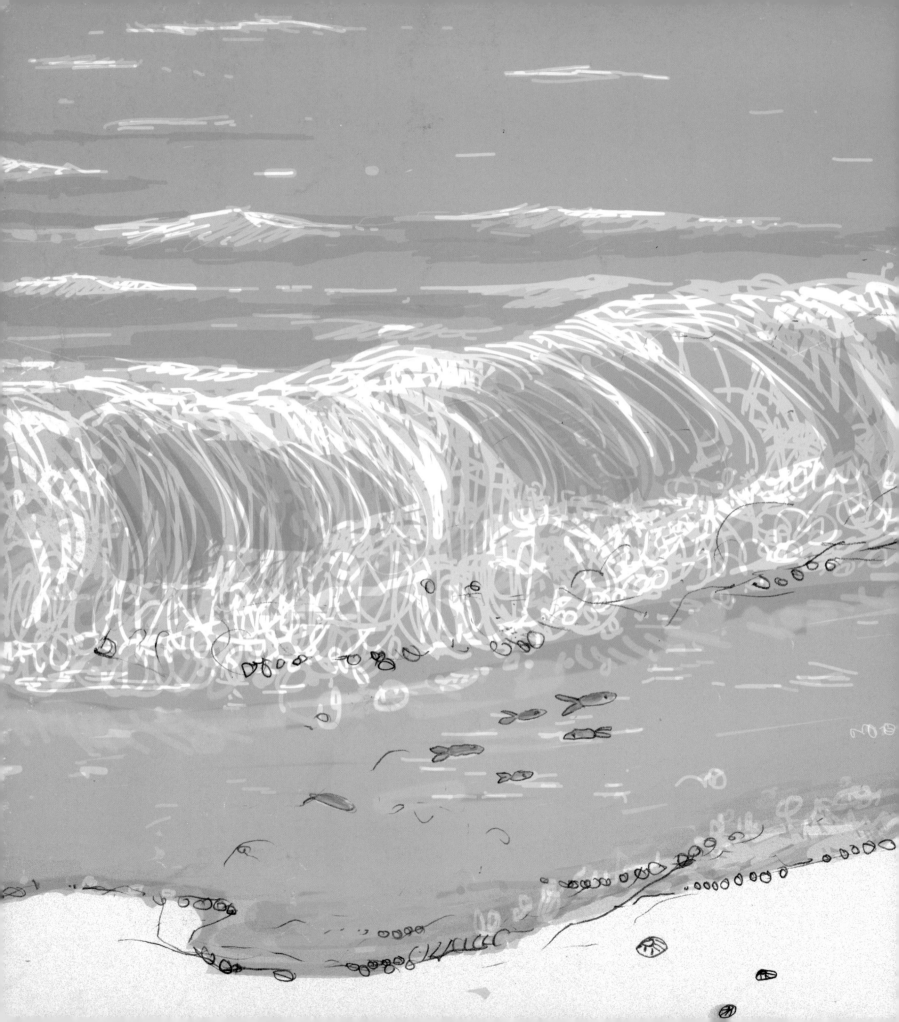

There are only the waves jumping and splashing.
They want to splash with somebody.

Splash!

The white waves splash
Anna Hibiscus.
Oh! Anna Hibiscus
splashes back.

Jump!

The white waves jump on
Anna Hibiscus.
Oh! Anna Hibiscus
jumps back.

Hee-hee!

The white waves laugh at Anna Hibiscus.
Oh! Anna Hibiscus laughs back.
"Hee-hee!
Hee-hee! Hee-hee!"

Chocolate hears Anna laughing.
She stops digging.
Angel shouts to Chocolate,
"Wait for me!"

Hee-hee! Hee-hee! Hee-hee!

Benz and Wonderful hear Anna laughing.
"Look! Let's go!" shouts Benz.
"Wondaful!" shouts Wonderful.

Joy, Clarity and Common Sense hear Anna laughing.

"We are not that old," says Clarity.

"We're not that busy," says Common Sense.

"Phones are so boring," says Joy. "Come on!"

Hee-hee!   Hee-hee!   Hee-hee!

Anna's mother and the aunties
hear Anna laughing.
"I'm hot!" says Anna's mother.
"Let's eat later," says
Auntie Joli.

Anna's father stops talking
when he hears Anna laughing.
"O-ya!" shouts Uncle Tunde.
"I'm coming!" shouts
Anna's father.

Anna's laughing is so loud
that Grandmother and Grandfather wake up.
"What are we waiting for?"
says Grandmother.
"Let's go!" says Grandfather.

Hee-hee! Hee-hee! Hee-hee! Hee-hee! Hee-hee! Hee-hee! Hee-hee!

Anna Hibiscus looks around.
She sees Chocolate and Angel
        and Benz and Wonderful and Clarity
            and Joy and Common Sense,
                and her mother and the aunties,

Hee-hee! Hee-hee! Hee-hee! Hee-hee! Hee-hee! Hee-hee!

and her father
and Uncle Tunde,
and even Grandmother
and Grandfather
all running down the hot yellow sand to –

SPLASH!
in the laughing waves.

"Hee-hee!"
laughs Anna Hibiscus.

"HEE-HEE!"
laughs the whole entire family.
"Hee-hee!" laugh the splashing waves.

Anna Hibiscus lives in Africa.
Amazing Africa.
Anna Hibiscus is amazing too.

Other Anna Hibiscus books by Atinuke and Lauren Tobia:

978-1-4063-1495-3

978-1-4063-0655-2

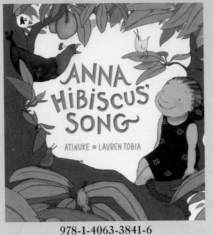

978-1-4063-3841-6

978-1-4063-2067-1

978-1-4063-2081-7

Also illustrated by Lauren Tobia:

978-1-4063-1508-0

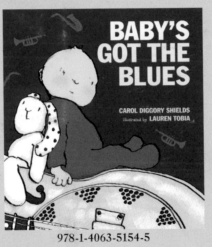

978-1-4063-5154-5

978-1-4063-1508-0

Atinuke was born in Nigeria and spent her childhood in both Africa
and the UK. Now a professional storyteller, she lives in Wales
with her husband and two sons.

Lauren Tobia lives in Bristol with her husband, two daughters
and two Jack Russells. When she's not busy illustrating books
she loves to dig on her allotment.

Available from all good booksellers

www.walker.co.uk